Why?

Written by **Yvette Gorman**
Illustrated by **Stephen Adams**

AuthorHouse™ UK Ltd.
1663 Liberty Drive
Bloomington, IN 47403 USA
www.authorhouse.co.uk
Phone: 0800.197.4150

Published by AuthorHouse 10/19/2016

ISBN: 978-1-5246-6163-2 (sc)
ISBN: 978-1-5246-6164-9 (e)

Print information available on the last page.

Any people depicted in stock imagery provided by Thinkstock are models,
and such images are being used for illustrative purposes only.
Certain stock imagery © Thinkstock.

This book is printed on acid-free paper.

authorHOUSE®

This story is dedicated to my Mam and Dad who have always supported my ideas no matter how crazy they may have been and for always believing in me.

When Sophie was a tiny girl, she didn't speak a lot,

She sat and played with all her toys, until she was filled with thought,

One day she asked a question, a big one it would seem,

Which required a thoughtful answer, from her parents is what I mean.

The answer sparked more questions,
Sophie needed to know more and more,
She asked and asked and asked and asked,
Until her mommy's ears where sore.

She asked things like "How's the sun so big?"
And "how does it stay up in the sky?"
And soon the answers alone weren't good enough,
Then she began just asking "Why?"

"Why is bread so soft at first, but then it gets quite hard?"

"And crackers are very hard yet easy to break in half?"

They were questions that couldn't be answered, but mom and dad tried their best,

But the more they answered, the more she asked,

And they never got a rest.

First she started waking early, 6 questions about why we dream,
She'd jump on the bed at 6am, then 5, then 4, then 3.

Her mam and dad began losing their marbles,
With the early mornings they just needed a break,
They prayed that the questions would soon stop,
But then Sophie started staying up late.

"Where do babies come from?".... "How do they get out?"

"How come they can't say a word, yet they are so loud when they shout?"

Soon Mom and dad began to get angry; they wanted the questions to stop,

The questions became too many to take, but do you think Sophie gave up? I think not,

She continued and continued and continued, pulling questions out of the air,

Until one day she felt a little strange from a reason she was unaware.

She went to her mum to ask her the question "What's love all about?

But just as she was about to ask no words would come out of her mouth,

She opened her mouth over and over but not a tiny sound did she make,

She looked at her mommy with tears in her eyes and her heart began to break.

What would she do without questions; the answers would be no more,

What was wrong with her, not a word could she say and she started to feel a bit sore,

Her mom just looked at her and smiled as she could see just what this was about,

She picked up Sophie and looked at her throat,

Then said "You've worn your voice box out"

Sophie began to cry and her mommy said "it's ok..

It's nothing to worry about you'll be fine in a couple of days".

Her mom thought then said "to hurry up your healing,
You've got to go to bed early and sleep the entire night,
And rest your voice, don't try to talk,
Before you know it you'll be just right."

So Sophie nodded and agreed,

For the questions to come back it was bed at 8oclock,

And she slept the whole night through,

She didn't budge and was silent as a rock.

Mom and dad got their sleep too,

They loved how much they could chill,

But after only two days,

They began to miss their questionable little girl.

So by day 3 Daddy started questioning her to encourage her to talk,

He asked her about the things she would know,

"Why do you dress your Barbie's like that?

"And why do you pull toy cars back to make them go?"

Day 4 mammy joined in on the asking

"Why is fruit the healthy option?"

"Why is chocolate considered a treat?"

"Why must we eat so many vegetables?"

"And a good selection of meat?"

Sophie of course didn't answer, she just continued to play with her toys,

Bed early every night, up late every day and she barely made any noise.

Mom and dad where getting pretty sad now,

Their house was far too quiet,

What could they do to get her to talk again?

But they got an idea and thought they would try it.

The next day which was day 7 when Sophie got down the stairs,

Mom and dad stood up and said together "Sophie tell us what love is?"

Sophie looked at them both like she was thinking,

Then with a smile on her pretty little face,

She opened her mouth to let the words fall out and said "well this is the case..."

"Love is when your soul is empty,

Because something is missing but you don't know what,

Then you have someone and your soul fills up,

And they become your every thought,

They do many things that annoy you,

But your love for them stays strong,

Because without them being themselves,

You don't feel like you quite belong,

So love is when you need someone,

No matter how annoying they can be,

My questions may have been far too much,

But when they stopped, you missed that part of me."

Lightning Source UK Ltd.
Milton Keynes UK
UKRC01n0928171116
287857UK00005B/44

9 781524 661632